That's Life, Lily

Valérie Dayre published her first book in 1989 and since then she has written over fifteen highly acclaimed children's books that have been translated into many languages. *C'est la vie, Lili* won the Prix Sorcière (the main French children's prize) and, in translation, the 2006 German Youth Literature Prize. It is the first of her novels to have been published in English.

That's Life, Lily

Valérie Dayre

translated by Theo Cuffe

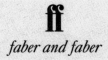

faber and faber

First published in 2008
by Faber and Faber Limited
3 Queen Square London WC1N 3AU

Printed in the UK by CPI Bookmarque, Croydon, CR0 4TD

A CIP record for this book
is available from the British Library

Liberté • Égalité • Fraternité
RÉPUBLIQUE FRANÇAISE

This book is supported by the French Ministry of Foreign
Affairs as part of the Burgess programme run by the
Cultural Department of the French Embassy in London
(www.frenchbooknews.com)

ISBN 978–0–571–23797–5

2 4 6 8 10 9 7 5 3 1

Contents

Going

Yesterday, as soon as we got here, they started to behave weirdly. A pretence of not being in a mood, of nothing being the matter, then stolen glances, frownings into corners, frownings at me, then at each other.

It took us a moment to get ourselves out of the boiling car. Mama had maintained all along that we should open the windows, but papa insisted that the air-conditioning was far better. For a hundred kilometres at least they had talked of nothing but temperature, open windows, closed windows. The windows were opened, closed and reopened, but after so much dithering no one knew any longer which was better. So they ended by asking my opinion. Which allowed them to change the subject, and to have a go at me, because I shrugged my shoulders and continued looking out at the countryside, saying I couldn't care less about the windows.

For the first hundred kilometres the problem

had not arisen. We had set out early. 'In the cool of the morning,' said papa. 'Three a.m. is the perfect time. The motorway will be empty.'

'So much for your predictions,' mama kept saying, over and over, for the three hours it took us to get to the motorway toll-gates, at more or less crawling pace, in the curving human swarm of holidaymakers.

After the toll-gates things were not much better, but at least the first obstacle had been passed.

We finally got to the motorway services around ten in the morning. 'Services'. I like that word.

It was already horribly hot, not to mention the fact that having the windows down while moving along at 40 k.p.h. was not making things any cooler.

I should add that, although in the end papa was proved right – in so far as all three of us were red-faced and drenched in perspiration – we discovered that the air-conditioning was not working anyway.

'I swear to God, what a car . . .!' muttered mama.

'So go and tell the manufacturer!' replied papa.

And because he was irritated, he drove into and slightly grazed the back of the car in front. Nothing serious, since we were only travelling at 15 k.p.h.

Everyone got out. The other driver came over, with his accident report form in hand. I could see how put out he was when he had to admit there was not even a scratch on his car.

'Oh well, these things happen,' said papa, trying to make light of it.

Mama was already busy commiserating with the other woman; they were grumbling in unison that the men never let them take the wheel.

As for me, when I saw the scowls on the faces of their two kids, I went back and sat in the car.

It should all have been settled quickly. If only the other guy hadn't told papa to drive in front, so that he could go behind, 'to avoid getting something in the behind' (accompanied by coarse guffawing). And given that we were likely to spend all day like this, 'arse to arse' (more sniggers), he preferred to keep an eye on our bumper rather than relying on papa to keep an eye on his.

'It comes to the same thing,' retorted papa. 'You'll just have someone else behind you all the way.'

'Yeah, but maybe someone a bit less dozy,' said the guy.

After which they exchanged a few more words, accompanied by shouts and gesticulations. I was no longer listening. Mama had got back into the car by now, satisfied that there would be no further developments. The woman from in front got into the back of their car, with her children. Mama turned to me and said:

'Lily, go and tell your father that we can go ahead of them. What difference does it make?'

I got out of the car and went up to papa. He and the other man could no longer hear each other shouting: all the cars behind them had started blowing their horns, on the pretext that we were blocking their way. It's true that the motorway had only two lanes at this point. What's more, we were stopped on the fast lane.

Fortunately I didn't have to try and make my voice, and the voice of reason, audible to papa. He was already on his way back to the car, purple-faced, hair all over the place. He got in, slammed the door and started revving the engine loudly in neutral.

The other driver was also behind his wheel by now, but hadn't pulled out. He had room to do so. But he was of course waiting for papa to pass in front, as had finally been agreed.

I got back into our car double-quick, since it seemed that in the excitement of the moment there was a strong chance of my being left behind.

But the problem, precisely, was how to pass in

front. No way of overtaking on the left, nor on the right: the other cars were now crawling past us in an uninterrupted stream.

'Get out and make them stop,' papa said to mama.

'Are you all right in the head?' shouted mama.

Papa slammed the steering wheel with his fist. Then he sighed heavily.

'OK, you drive and I'll deal with the rest.'

He got out. The guy in the other car poked his head out of the driver's window, beaming with hilarity.

'It's a tough one!' he called out after papa.

Papa pretended to ignore this, but I heard him mutter a very rude word as he went past my open window.

He planted himself in the middle of the slow lane, a little way behind our car, and raised his hand traffic-policeman style.

Mama wriggled over behind the steering wheel.

The chorus of hooting horns in the slow lane now joined forces with the hooting horns of the fast lane.

As she was letting out the clutch mama stalled the car. I don't think it was her fault – the engine had probably overheated. Or at least that's what she told papa when he came back, all exasperation.

Slyly, the cars in the slow lane had begun moving forwards again. We had to start all over from the beginning. First we had to get the car going, which was not obvious. Papa took over. He was getting redder and redder in the face.

He handed the wheel back to mama, grudgingly, and went back to policing the egoists in the slow lane. This time mama did not make a mess of it, and we found ourselves passing the guy in front, in the slow lane. But when mama tried to swing back into the fast lane, in front of the guy in front, so that he could go behind us, things got really tricky.

'A total degenerate,' as papa explained to us afterwards.

Just when mama was changing lanes, after signalling with her indicator, the other guy suddenly started up and shot off. Just like that. Mama very nearly went into his side.

Which was when we heard wailings coming from behind: we had forgotten papa.

As if on purpose, the traffic had in the meantime started moving again. Maybe because we had, after all, been blocking both lanes. There were now a clear three hundred yards of boiling tarmac ahead of us. Three hundred yards without a car.

After picking up papa, however, we again found ourselves right behind the guy from in front. Having shot off, he had only advanced a few yards and was now waiting for us, laughing.

'I won't stand for much more of this,' said papa.

I made the mistake of suggesting that, since we were now in the slow lane, we could keep going, and leave the guy in the other lane, neither in front nor behind. Papa turned around and looked at me with a furious expression.

There were, as I said before, three hundred yards of empty motorway in front of us, which had now become four hundred yards. Papa accelerated, and the car lurched forwards.

However, right on cue, the guy from in front also accelerated, and both cars now found themselves racing side by side, as if glued to one another.

'A total degenerate, this guy,' repeated papa.

In the other car, the kids were sticking their tongues out at me and making faces. I turned away. It was idiotic, but I was close to tears. Because I was upset and irritated? I don't know. I wanted to see something beautiful. I looked around. There was nothing.

The contest did not last long. Papa had 'more balls', as he put it afterwards.

The guy from in front braked first, so as not to run into the platoon of cars up ahead, and papa made the most of this opportunity by cutting in front of him. We now found ourselves ahead, with the guy from in front behind us. With the result, however, that papa had been forced to brake sharply to avoid the other cars, whereas the other guy did not have time to do likewise. So he went into the back of our car.

It was at this point that mama had her fit of hysterics.

We were in front, after all, just as the guy from in front had wanted, to avoid having his rear bumper dented. Except that now he had a smashed front bumper instead.

At which point he and papa started to draw up the accident report for the insurance. I tried to calm mama; the other woman brought her a glass of water, which was nice of her. She at least did not have fits of hysterics, but she looked somehow grey, like a switched-off lamp.

The two kids had rolled themselves into a ball on the floor of the back seat, like hedgehogs. They were no longer visible, no longer audible.

I had seen their father turn around, just before getting out of his car for the accident report, and box each of them soundly on the ears. He nearly boxed his wife in the process, since she was also sitting in the back. But he stopped himself in time. Because he saw how grey she looked, I suppose.

The traffic was held up once again for the accident report, naturally. But things were sorted out in the end. Two motorbike police stopped on the hard shoulder; they managed to get both cars to park alongside the crash barrier, and they took charge of the report, since papa and the other guy could not agree on whose fault it was. The guy behind – originally the guy in front – refused to share any responsibility, claiming that papa had cut in on him, and from the wrong side moreover.

I don't know how exactly it was all resolved. Mama recovered her calm.

More than ever I was on the edge of tears. Less and less could I understand why.

All of this happened yesterday, and it already feels so long ago. A day has passed, and a night. And these were only ordinary everyday goings-on.

Afterwards, everything really changed.

By the time we reached the motorway services everyone had calmed down. Papa had ranted and raved for a good while. But the more he considered the matter – not least the humiliation of having had to blow into a breathalyser – the more 'philosophical' he felt, as he told us several times.

Which did not prevent him from accelerating each time he saw a car ahead that resembled the guy in front's car. Fortunately, we did not cross paths with the guy in front again. No doubt by now he was well ahead of us, given that we had been obliged yet again to pull over onto the hard shoulder.

This time it was my fault. I felt sick. I spent quite some time vomiting. Papa cursed. I was 'holding them up no end'.

So, having arrived at the motorway services at last, safe and sound, we all got out of the car with no air-conditioning and a dented rear (though the boot still opened without any problem). All was well.

Except that they both had this peculiar look in their eyes, as I said at the beginning. Something shifty and un-straightforward.

'Look how grand it is here!' said mama. 'It's like a proper town.'

Oddly emotional suddenly, she pulled me towards her and hugged me tightly.

Papa looked at us tenderly, rested a limp hand on my head, discreet but loving, and in a slightly hoarse voice (for he too was overcome by what he was looking at) said:

'A village, not a town,' correcting her. 'A real village. And all of it along a bridge . . . all of it suspended! The things they can do these days with architecture . . . it's amazing! Nobody ever says it out loud, but in five hundred years this is how our century will be remembered. It rivals anything, even . . . even Venice!'

'Ohhh, Venice . . . when are you taking me to Venice?' mama now crooned, as she clung to his neck. She had let go of me; clearly it wasn't me who would be taking her to Venice. Papa went on with his soliloquy.

'I don't know if one can justly compare a motorway services to Venice. But the twentieth century had this great virtue, that unlike all the preceding centuries it made no attempt to incorporate the beautiful, the permanent, into its creations. I for one prefer this absence of pretension, this humility of man confronted by a cosmos against which he no longer tries to measure himself. He has at last accepted his littleness, his insignificance. No one will ever again dare to build a cathedral. From now on mankind will content itself with tracing gestures, cries and whispers swallowed by the dark, as the vapour trail of an aeroplane fades into the ether.'

I looked at papa. I tried to detect some trace of this humility in his expression, this absence of pretension he was praising to the skies. But I could see nothing of the kind. I looked away.

I for one would like to go on building cathedrals.

'So, when are you taking me to Venice?' mama continued dreamily. Still clinging to his neck, she stamped her foot petulantly on the ground, and the heel of her sandal got stuck in the tarmac, which had gone soft in the heat.

'Soon. You'll see,' papa promised, giving her waist a squeeze. 'Maybe even this winter. Jacques in the office gave me a fantastic travel brochure. Fabulous prices.'

Mama still had her foot suspended. She bent

down to extract her sandal from the sticky black tar, and was gallantly lifted by papa, sandal too, and transported to a patch of grassy border.

'Venice . . .' she continued crooning, making gondolier-type paddling movements against his chest.

This is their game of the moment. He sings 'O sole mio' and she rocks to and fro, whispering to him that the chilled champagne awaits them in the palace.

Mama calls this 'the right to dream', and she says that for the right to champagne and a palace, and gondolas, she would willingly join the revolution.

At school I am taught that the revolution is when you have no bread and no liberty. Mama must be a bit out of touch. She claims moreover to have joined the revolution when she was seventeen. Often such words sound false on her lips, or on papa's.

'At a party, one night,' she explained to me, on the subject of revolution. 'For the right to make love before getting married.'

And the right to stop me from coming into this world until she decided I should. For a long time I used to think that she carried me around for ten years in her womb, drinking non-stop champagne and throwing confetti.

'God, you can be so reactionary!' is what she always says to me. And then papa joins in, on cue: 'All children are reactionary. Frightful little fascists.'

'I don't know why, but they seem so much more mature for their age than we were at ours,' replies mama. 'Look at your daughter, how seriously she reflects on the world, how much she thinks about the future. I don't know if we've spoilt her too much or not enough . . .'

At such moments I find myself in the crossfire of two pairs of eyes, sombre and suspicious. No, not suspicious, but curious, a bit like the bulging eyeball of the biology teacher when she looks through the microscope.

I have parents who ask themselves many questions on my account.

As for this business of revolution – no, I will have to give it further thought. One thing is clear: it irritates me.

As we walked through the parked cars, they were still discussing Venice.

'Listen', said papa finally, with a sigh. 'The sea, for this year, is not bad going. Isn't that what you wanted? The beach, the warm water, nothing to do, no one else to worry about, nothing to think about . . .'

They both worship the idea of nothing to think about, as if they usually spent their time locked in thought. Which is not my impression, although I may be mistaken. As for worrying about others . . .

Mama looked at me, gave a meaningful little cough in my direction and unhooked herself from papa's neck. We were at the bottom of the stairs leading to the cafeteria and shops. The air smelled of tar, chips, chewing gum. It was hot. I waded through the litter and empty packaging. The cars on the motorway made a constant, deafening noise.

A village, yes, papa.

I turned back towards the car park jammed with cars, their roof-racks groaning beneath suitcases, bicycles, windsurfing boards. Doors slamming, people red in the face, people sweating, short-tempered.

My attention was caught by three fat bottoms wedged into fluorescent multicoloured shorts, nothing else visible above their podgy white legs. Or at least I could see nothing: they were all leaning into the back of a car, parked near the cafeteria stairs.

'Come on, down you get,' a man's voice was saying. 'Time for dindins. Come on, there's a good boy.'

'I told you all along that this would turn into a saga,' bellowed the woman next to him. 'It would have been better to get it over and done with in Montrouge.'

'And find him sitting on the doorstep when we got back home?'

'Well, so what is the Society for the Protection of Animals for? They'd have picked him up!'

'You know as well as I do that they keep them for five minutes before giving them an injection. When they're not trying to track down the owners!'

'He might at least have got himself caught by the people who sell them for experiments,' said the child who was with them.

He was a boy of about my age. Then he said:

'Mama, when we get back in September, the next one will be a different colour, right?'

'I don't care as long as it's short-haired', exclaimed the woman.

'It's true,' muttered the man. 'He always stinks.'

'I hope you're not suggesting we should have paid for him to be groomed before we left!'

'In any case, never again a dog with long hairs. When you think of what his grooming has cost . . . Hang on a minute! No way! I bet the bastard is going to piss on the back seat!'

'Not on the seat!' screamed the woman. 'The new seat-covers!'

There followed a tensely expectant silence. The woman was the first to break it. The danger had seemingly passed.

'So, is this mongrel going to get out of the car or not? God, you are pathetic sometimes,' she told her husband.

She straightened up. Mascara was running down her cheeks. With a martial step she went to the car boot, opened it, and got out a battered-looking plastic ball.

'Hey! Who's got the ball-ball? Who's got the ball-ball?' she started chanting. The boy joined in, yelling: 'Ball-ball! Where's the ball-ball?' His mother threw it to him. He threw it back. So as not to miss out on the fun, the husband now chimed in: 'Look at the ball-ball! Where's the ball? What a pretty ball!'

They were no longer blocking my view of the inside of the car. I could see the dog sitting on the back seat, on which he had made the big mistake of not pissing. A big black dog. With long hair, it was true.

He cocked his head, watching the others play ball, his ears pricking up.

The idiot, I said to myself, he's going to jump.

Down he went, and sprang out of the car, trying to intercept the ball as it was tossed between his owners.

All three of them laughed as the dog launched himself with scarcely credible bounds, and comically perilous leaps, his spine bent right back.

But now the boy aimed the ball wide, and the father pretended to be fooled by the dummy shot. It rolled between the parked cars, the dog in pursuit.

The traitors got back into the car, in less time than it takes to write this sentence. The doors slammed shut, the windows rolled up, the engine roared, and the car pulled away with a screeching of tyres.

The dog had reappeared between two parked cars, his nose rapidly sniffing along the hot tarmac after the ball. When he looked up and saw his owners disappearing inside their vehicle, he stopped dead in his tracks, his forelegs apart, with a forlorn expression. And when the car had gone, he barked just once. Then he turned around, looking at the ground.

I kept watching, and now he made himself flat as a pancake and slid under a car, then reappeared immediately with the ball in his mouth. Now he started to run with long strides after his owners' car, the ball held tightly between his teeth. From where I was standing, I could no longer see his owners. They had gone.

The dog kept chasing.

A car jammed on its brakes to avoid him, then a van towing a caravan jammed on its brakes behind the car.

I feared the worst, but then I glimpsed once more the big shape of the dog stretching out as it raced along at full tilt. Not covered in blood on the tarmac of the car park.

When I walked back towards the stairs, there was no one at the entrance to the suspended village. Or rather, no one that I was looking for.

I can imagine the expression on the faces of the parents of Tom Thumb or Hansel and Gretel, when they see their children coming back for the first time: the expression of people who are hungry and cold, and have no hope of not being hungry or cold one day.

This was not the look of my parents, when they suddenly saw me reappear beside the car. Mama went red in the face and burst into nervous laughter.

'You monkey! Where have you been? We were waiting for you.'

Like hell they were. From the stairs of the cafeteria, I had become aware of them threading their way between the cars, bent triple so as not to be noticed. Or at least, not noticed by me. But I could get my bearings on them merely by looking at the other people in the car park, who kept lowering their heads as they walked along, as if following some bizarre activity taking place at their feet.

I had run around on the other side, so as to get to the car before them. A practical joke. Since they are always telling me I have no sense of humour.

I slid into the back seat without saying a word. Two concerned faces were now framed in the open window.

'Did you have a pee, Lily?'

'Are you hungry, Lily?'

'Do you want to go and get yourself something in the shop over there, or a CD?'

'A cassette?'

'A floral-printed T-shirt?'

'An ice-cream?'

'A yoghurt?'

'Some biscuits?'

'A pie?'

Or a ball-ball, perhaps? Why not.

Finally, mama said, 'Oh, my throat is so dry, and I've forgotten to buy a bottle of water! Would you be an angel, Lily . . .?'

I shook my head and stopped looking at them. I said nothing. My heart was beating very quickly. It was hot on the back seat and I wanted to pee all over it, like a dog in the grip of blank fear.

I almost told them that next time they should get themselves one that is stupider – one that was born yesterday, one that came down with the last shower of rain. It would be easier for them.

I saw the dog again.

He looks dirty, and very thin and tired.

He came back today. I'd have spotted him sooner otherwise.

'You OK?' I asked.

'Not so good.'

'Are you hungry?'

'Not much.'

'Did you chase after them for long?'

He did not seem surprised that I knew his story. That's how dogs are.

'I lost the ball-ball. I let it drop, and then a lot of cars went past. I couldn't follow it.'

'Why did you come back here?'

He shook himself all over. His four paws were spread out as he stretched himself, so that his hollow stomach almost touched the ground. Then he gathered himself together, legs very straight, very proud, and made as if to forget my question.

I did not press him for an answer. I wanted to

stroke him, and put my arm round his neck. But I did not dare. We hardly knew each other.

If he stays around for a while I will tell him that it is called a ball.

On Monday I did not pee on the back seat after all.

My parents walked off a little distance from the car, in which I remained seated. I suppose they were reviewing the situation.

I watched. I couldn't hear what they were saying, but mama had that crumpled look she has when she is about to break down, because 'life is impossible and the world unspeakable'. Those are her words, every time.

I could see the moment coming when I'd hear papa shout the magic word:

'VENICE!'

At which mama's face would uncrumple and she would stop wanting to cry.

Two years ago, they had had a different magic word. Less powerful than Venice, it had to be said twice for its full effect to be felt: BORA-BORA.

But in the end they had 'done' Bora-Bora in eight days; after which the magic words were

27

heard only on long evenings of tedium, when one gets out the holiday slides. They needed to find a new word, 'because', as papa explained, 'everything wears out and everything passes. Even life's pleasures.'

In the bathroom new brochures replaced the old ones, and on the coffee table in front of the all-leather sofa. We passed from bright sun and palm trees to the bluish fog of the lagoon and the masks of the carnival.

On Monday I did not tell them that they should have got themselves one that was born yesterday, one that came down with the last shower of rain. I was suffocating from the heat, so I got out of the car.

I walked in the direction of the cafeteria.

If they had asked me, I would have said that I was going to get a ball-ball.

They asked me nothing. I made things easier for them. I did not come back.

I did not go to Bora-Bora.

I don't want to be taken to Venice.

And what's more, I do not feel like crying.

The car park is even more crowded, and has hardly been less than full since the start of the week. Cars circle for hours trying to find a space, and just now two men nearly came to blows over the only spot that is out of the sun, where a miserable poplar casts a bit of shade on the yellow grass beneath.

The dog and I sat all morning in the shade next to the cold drinks and hot-dog shack. The dog dozed, while I read.

Solange gave me a book yesterday. She gives me something every day. Her first present was this notebook in which I am writing. Along with the pen.

After I'd spent an hour in her shop, she could see clearly that it wasn't the sweets that interested me. Not as a priority. She gave me some all the same.

She worries about me. She feels responsible.

I was outside her shop the first evening, as she

was switching off the lights and lowering the metal shutters.

It was eleven o'clock – 23.03 according to the clock with the numbers made out of little luminous red dots.

'What are you doing there, little one?'

I wanted to pretend I was a deaf-mute, as I used to do with Sophie, to make fun of people's expressions in the street. But I was tired and was beginning to get hungry. It was just as hot as during the day.

I felt I was on the point of crumpling, but I did not want her taking me anywhere, even if she had nice eyes and looked big and maternal in her flowery dress.

'Where are your parents?'

I looked around.

On the other side of the corridor, behind large plate-glass windows with trellises and plastic plants, a lot of people were at tables eating, with yellow or green heads depending on how close they were to the neon lights. With a nod, I gestured towards the tables.

'They're in the restaurant?

I nodded.

'And you have finished eating?'

I indicated that this was the case.

30

'Well, you shouldn't be wandering about alone. It's a big place, and you might get lost. Go on, run along to your parents. Otherwise they'll get worried.'

I smiled as prettily as I knew how, making a pretence of returning to the restaurant.

When she turned her back and bent down to lock the shutters, I darted into the toilets.

I stayed there for a while.

Each time someone came in, I pressed the button on the hand-drier.

That night, my first night, I slept on the ground in one of the toilet cubicles, the cleanest I could find. I was awoken next morning by the cleaning woman banging on the doors, making a racket with her broom. I had just enough time to stand up, pull the chain, and leave the cubicle, with a big smile for the cleaner.

Mama says I have a devil of a smile, and that if I employed it more often around the house, life would be a lot more pleasant.

I am stopping writing now. The dog has just woken up. We need to go and find something to eat.

Solange is not under the impression that my parents have been eating solidly for six days in the restaurant; she merely supposes that my father or mother works in the self-service canteen, and that they bring me here every day because there's no convenient grandmother to leave me with.

It's true about there being no grandmother. As for the rest, I do not try to correct her. It would upset her, and she would worry even more about me.

She thinks my parents neglect me. So she does what she can. Every day she gives me something. Soon I'll need to ask her for a bag to hold all the presents she has given me. In the meantime I hide them in a black bin-liner that I borrowed from the cleaning woman in charge of the storage room. I regularly change the hiding place, so no one notices my bag. They would lose no time in rummaging amongst my things.

At midday Solange is in her shop waiting for me. I arrive, I say good morning, we chat, and

32

then she asks me what's on today's menu in the cafeteria. The dishes are always the same, but every day she hopes there will be something new. Solange believes that hope keeps life going. And because she is fond of food, her hope lives between her tongue and her palate. She has decided that, with my mother or father working in the kitchens, I must know what's cooking in there. I do not disabuse her.

So, at eleven-thirty every morning I am in the kitchens. I lift the lids, on the lookout for what smells passably good.

Thinking that I am under instructions from Solange, they have quickly got used to me, down there amongst the greasy ovens. They smile at me, make jokes, call me 'chef', or 'food inspector', or 'the taster'.

And they put a few mouthfuls of each dish on a plate for me. I try everything, and say if it's good or not. And I let them know that all this is giving me an appetite. Then someone says, 'Well, it's a healthy illness,' and they serve me a plate of my preferred dish.

If I find nothing to my taste, they'll throw a steak onto the smoking hotplate. A quick turn on each side, and the steak is served up on a large plate heaped with chips.

I go and sit down at a table in the dining room. The dog is waiting for me. On the busiest days, he keeps a place for me. We share the steak and chips, or whatever is on the plate.

But I realise that I am telling you a lot of un-interesting things. Besides, I am tired.

Sunday was horrible.

I can't remember why I interrupted what I was writing, the day before the day before yesterday.

The dog likes meat with gravy.

But on gravy days we make a lot of mess, the pair of us, and I am nervous until he has licked clean the plate that I put on the floor beside him while Armelle's back is turned.

Every lunchtime Armelle clears the plates from the tables, and goes over them with a cloth so that the scraps fall on the floor. In the evenings it's Claudine. Which allows me and the dog to come back for dinner without seeming greedy.

The dog eats like a horse. He is not as thin as the day he came back from his marathon on the motorway.

He asked me to wash him if I thought he smelled too bad. I don't think he does, but I have a feeling he likes to keep up appearances.

So I shampooed him, taking advantage of a sprinkler that is used to water the small patch of grass at the edge of the car park. In the process I got myself lathered in suds from head to foot. It was nice.

Afterwards I changed my clothes. I put on the dress that Solange brought for me yesterday. Too small for her daughter, she said, adding that she preferred to give it to me rather than her niece, whom she doesn't really like that much. But it was obvious that the pairs of 'Petit Bateau' knickers included in the bag had had no previous owner. On one of them Solange had forgotten to remove the nylon thread that holds the price tag.

When I put on the dress, Solange told me to give her my trousers and shirt, on the pretext that one was torn and the other had a loose button.

Next morning, they were cleaned, ironed, and mended, and they smelled of lavender.

Tomorrow, I will continue to describe life here, in detail, because everything is going well. Here, where I have been for nine days. Nine days as of tomorrow morning, at ten o'clock.

Everything is fine.

There was a big storm last night. The dog and I had to go and sleep inside. Normally we stay outside, so as not to have to hear the music, which never stops. We find the noise of the cars preferable.

And the dog keeps me warm.

I think I also keep the dog warm, a bit too warm, but he puts up with it all the same.

In the electric light the people looked ugly, incredibly ugly. We were hidden against a partition wall, behind some tubs of plastic plants. We didn't sleep much, so today we keep dozing off.

Exactly the same as on Sunday, there was suddenly this guy leaning over me, trying to start a conversation:

'He looks like a nice dog, your dog.'

And he began to stretch his hand towards the muzzle of the dog, to show me that the dog was really nice, that the guy was really nice, that I was probably also really nice.

Just like on Sunday. Incredible.

But this was a different guy. The other one had been younger.

And the dog bared his teeth, just as he did on Sunday, a mere snapping of jaws in empty space, just enough to make the guy understand that he'd rung the wrong doorbell, that he was not among nice people.

'Hey there, what a temper!' said the guy.

He must have learnt his lines from the other guy, word for word.

At which point it was my cue to speak, so I said:

'That's right. In fact, on Sunday he ate a bloke. A bigger bloke than you.'

The guy gave a smile, as of an indulgent father-figure, and proceeded to ignore the dog, who proceeded to ignore the guy.

'So you were here already on Sunday, then?'

'Obviously,' I said. 'My parents work here.'

I set both parents to work, at this point, just to add to the overall effect. It's as well that I have this set piece prepared, for each occasion that I am pestered. The guy straightened up (he had been crouching to make conversation with me) and looked around him, with a sort of lifeless smile.

'Well, that's great. Yeah. That's good. That's . . . Yep.'

And then he was gone.

Just like on Sunday. The next time, the next guy, I'll ask him straight out whether he's lost and if he'd like me to call the police for him.

In the kitchen they take me for Solange's daughter, or niece, since I come for her tray every lunchtime. I shout to the girl at the till: 'For Solange!' By this time I have already eaten my lunch, but I always find on the tray an ice cream or a tart or a mousse that is not for Solange, since she goes without dessert in the hope of getting thin. Someone in the kitchen puts this treat on the tray, and the girl at the till takes care never to add it to Solange's bill. I checked that this was the case, because the first two days I was there I felt embarrassed to treat myself to a dessert at the expense of this woman who was already showering me with presents, even if it meant I was keeping her company during her lunch.

The dog does not like desserts. If he is still hungry after a meal, he goes and positions himself in front of the snack bar outside, and waits for some toddler to drop his hot dog. It always happens. And the toddler always wants to pick it up, and the grown-up always says, 'Leave it, it's covered in dirt!' and everyone is happy to watch the dog pounce on it.

Because no one likes waste. To avoid which there is charity, which was probably invented specifically to deal with the problem.

It was on account of charity that I received my first slap in the face.

It happened just after the Armenian earthquake.

Mama had watched the news reports on TV; she was shattered by it all. Wanting to help the victims, she began turning the apartment upside down to find something to give them. She spent an entire Saturday afternoon occupied in this way.

When papa came back from his body-building session he could hardly open the front door, so crammed was the hallway with what mama had found for the Armenians.

Which included:

— her cast-off suits, or suits that no longer fitted her, or no longer pleased her;
— old kitchen utensils, made of zinc, badly dented, three-quarters of them with missing handles;
— canvas suitcases with worn-out corners;

- my old toys;
- board games no longer playable because individual pieces or cards were missing;
- ill-assorted dinner plates;
- socks belonging to papa, with the elastic gone;
- papa's old ties;
- his threadbare jacket, whose lining had gone;
- a bottle of stale cologne;
- an old pair of gloves with pompoms;
- more pompoms, this time candy pink, attached to winter earmuffs (mama was especially pleased with this contribution, it being dreadfully cold in Armenia); my infant bedspread, so frayed that you can see through it.

Along with many other things that I cannot now remember. Oh yes, plus a nearly empty bottle of antiseptic cream, and two rolls of sticking plaster that had lost their adhesive (not forgetting how many casualties there were during the quake).

'We'll call SOS Armenia and tell them to come and collect it all,' explained mama when she saw papa's look of astonishment.

'Yes . . .' he replied. 'That sounds like be a good idea.'

I suddenly found myself blurting out: 'You may as well call the dustmen. This is not a donation, it's a rubbish heap. You are only giving them what you want to throw out. And sticking plaster is not what people need when they've been crushed beneath their houses!'

For which I received a prompt slap in the face from mama, who then went and shut herself in her room.

I was stunned, and stood holding back my tears.

Papa led me into the sitting room, and sat me down on the sofa, where he assumed an anxious and solemn face to explain to me that mama must be very tired after her tidying up, and that it was always good to give away one's things.

'Because we have too much and have been waiting for ages to get rid of it all?' I asked.

'It is entirely to your mother's credit that she did not throw it all away, since it can now be of use to others.'

'But most of these things can't be used any longer.'

I did not continue. My voice was trembling too much.

The next morning, Sunday, when I got up, mama was singing in the corridor and making up parcels. She had gone out to the supermarket,

which is open on Sunday mornings, to get cardboard boxes in which to put all her donations.

There were two piles, two columns reaching
up to the ceiling.

We had to wait until Wednesday evening before
two gentlemen from SOS Armenia finally came
round to collect them.

'They're not exactly in a hurry, are they?' said
mama, by now in a state of exasperation. 'When
you think of how they go on and on at us about it
being an emergency.'

I could see her getting more and more grim-
faced each time she negotiated the cluttered
corridor.

Finally they showed up. The situation was
indeed an 'emergency', as they explained politely
to mama, but there had been a lot to do during
the past few days, and she was not alone in
wanting to contribute to the international effort.

Hearing those words 'international effort',
mama flushed with a sort of confused pleasure,
and said it was no problem their leaving her with
a cluttered corridor for so long; after all, she was
still fortunate enough to have a roof over her
head!

In short, it was all proceeding splendidly – 'all
for the best, in the best of all worlds'. My grand-

father was forever quoting this phrase. He said it was from Voltaire, and that it was ironical.

But now grandfather was no longer with us, and all does not go quite so well in the best of all possible worlds . . .

To cut a long story short, when the two blokes from SOS Armenia saw the piles of boxes, they said, 'So what's all this?'

'Lots of things,' said mama. 'Warm clothes, crockery, medication, food . . .'

She had also found a dozen tins (pâtés, canned fruit, spinach) at the back of the kitchen cupboard: the sort of supplies that are always bought in for those evenings when you forget to plan for dinner, those 'stop-gap' occasions. Except that, in the event, a better alternative is always found. Not least in our household, where there is a freezer stuffed with things a good deal more appetising than tinned pâté.

When the SOS men rang the doorbell I hid in the bathroom, leaving the door onto the corridor slightly ajar, so I would miss none of the conversation.

When I heard mama magically transforming her hotchpotch into 'warm clothes' and 'medication', I had to restrain myself from crying out that this was not true.

46

In any case, the two guys must have learnt a thing or two during the ten days they had spent gathering the donations of well-meaning citizens.

'Can we look?' said one of them.

Mama's voice rose a few octaves.

'Well, I have packed it all so . . . carefully, and into different categories – must you really undo everything? You can do that when you get it home!'

They stood their ground.

In the bathroom I had to put my hand in front of my mouth to stifle my giggles.

After opening three boxes, the SOS men had not made a single comment, and silence reigned in the corridor.

Then: 'Can you not write us a cheque instead?' asked the first man, the one who had spoken earlier.

'Oh, money!' retorted mama stiffly. 'Of course. It always comes down to money. Is that all that counts? And what about human fellow-feeling . . .?'

But she did not continue in this vein. I don't know whether she stopped of her own accord, or if they indicated to her that she was wasting her time.

Then the one who had not spoken so far added, in an even voice: 'A small amount would do. Whatever you can give. Ten euros . . .'

I'm not sure how in the end mama sent them packing, back to their 'fund-raising', as she called it. I no longer heard their voices; the door simply closed curtly behind them.

And at that moment I was ashamed.

The cardboard boxes stayed in the corridor for a month. Then, with Christmas approaching, mama insisted that some humanitarian organisation was bound to want to come and take them.

She spent hours on the phone. She tried everything: the third world, the fourth world on our doorstep ('we have our own poor too, you know') – she probably tried the best of all worlds, and any other worlds out there. But no one had time to come for the boxes. She was sickened by the whole business.

One morning, very early, a rag-and-bone man finally rang the doorbell.

After taking a quick look in the boxes, he asked mama for a hundred euros: 'Listen, there's nothing worth keeping amongst this junk. It's all for the rubbish tip. And it's I who have to pay for throwing this crap into the tip.'

Mama wrote him a silent cheque.

'You could have sent it to the Armenians, your

cheque. Even ten euros, they'd have been grateful
. . .' I said to her later.

'I'd have given them ten million, if only they'd
taken away those boxes!'

When papa asked her where the boxes had
finally gone, she put an end to all further discus-
sion by announcing: 'No more charity.'

She was disgusted, but in the end, she added, it
was worth paying a hundred euros to discover
that it was no longer possible to do a good turn in
this world.

Nevertheless, on Christmas evening, when the
woman who lived below us knocked on our door,
very drunk, because her man, likewise drunk, had
thrown her out, mama informed her that she
couldn't come in: that the whole family was here,
that my three cousins were spending the night,
that the apartment was simply too small. She
suggested to the woman that she try the hostel for
the homeless, three blocks away.

'Besides, she stank,' explained mama when the
neighbour had gone.

Mama has a better grasp of what she sees on
television than what she sees in real life. And the
screen blocks off all unpleasant odours.

We had never actually set eyes on the woman

before. We had only heard her. Sometimes she and her husband shout at each other, and quarrel, after which nothing more is heard except the dull sound of blows and stifled cries.

Then papa or mama phones to ask them to make less noise; we did not come and live 'in a respectable apartment block in order to put up with this sort of thing!'

Also on that Christmas evening I vomited, and mama scolded me, saying that I must have eaten too many chocolates.

I don't know if I'd have wanted the woman to stay with us. It's true, she smelt strongly of alcohol. Her eyes fastened on people and things without seeing them, and not for a moment did they take in the Christmas tree with all its lights.

I think she made us all a little afraid, as if she were a threat . . . But a threat of what?

What was I talking about, before all these stories?

Oh yes, the dog and the hot dogs.

The dog, as I was saying, wolfs down the frank-furters dropped by the children. They fall in the dirt, and the parents stop their kids from picking them up.

As well as being clumsy and obedient, as the dog explained to me, children have the good sense not to put mustard on sausages. He doesn't mind eating 'hot dogs', because he knows it's just a stupid expression for a piece of bread crammed with a frankfurter. But he doesn't like mustard.

I have written nothing in my notebook since Thursday. I had had enough of setting down memories from the time when I lived with my parents. I'd prefer to have memories that make me feel good, that leave me with regrets.

The things I've remembered, they can make me cry, but not with regret.

This Sunday, something disagreeable happened again. I mislaid the plastic bag in which I keep all my things. I don't know if I really lost it, or if I forgot where I'd hidden it, or if someone found it and took it. Anyway, instead of retrieving it from among the plastic flowers in the third tub along in front of the cafeteria, I eventually found it in the toilets, carefully perched on top of the partition between two cubicles.

What is especially worrying is that this cannot be a practical joke played by the dog. He could have taken the bag from the tub of fake flowers, but he could not have balanced it on top of the partition.

52

He claims he saw no one with my plastic bag. In future I am going to have to be a lot more careful.

After recovering it, however, I reread all of my journal, and wondered what someone coming upon it by chance would make of it. It was then that I realised I had only quite nasty things to say about my parents. I don't know what has come over me – I have plenty of good memories of them, even warm memories.

To be fair, I ought to write down some of these too. The only thing is, I don't know where to begin. I will think this over. And since I am about halfway through my notebook and halfway through my holidays, the second part of my journal will be all about how my parents love me and how I love them. I ought to take more time to think, so as not to write down any old rubbish.

My second Sunday at the motorway services was almost as dreadful as my first.

Solange does not work on Sundays, except, she explained to me, the busiest Sundays. For example, she opened her shop on Sunday, 29 July, just before I arrived.

In a sense, I prefer Solange not to be there on Sundays. She would be amazed to find me there.

On Saturday evening, that is to say my second Saturday, she asked me a lot of questions. Solange is never inquisitive, which is the reason she has taken so long to try and find out a little more about me.

I ended by telling her that it was my father who works in the kitchens. And in case she decided to make his acquaintance, I added that he's a foreigner and speaks only Serbo-Croat. I was sure she could not possibly know Serbo-Croat.

I also said that he has problems, and prefers not to have to talk about me with people. That I am a burden to him. That mama – who is French – left me with him on 31st July and went off to Venice.

Listening to me, Solange's eyes were full of tears.

I felt annoyed, and ashamed of myself.

To console her, I added that my father also has Sundays off, that he takes me out all day, to a restaurant and then to the cinema, and then again to another restaurant and another cinema; that my father is very gentle in spite of his problems, that I do not know him very well because he has never lived with mama and me, but that we manage nonetheless, that we eat our meals here, and sleep in his apartment in town, where I have my own bed on the sofa, and that the only problem is that he has no washing machine, which is why it is so incredibly nice of her to clean my clothes and repair them. I told her all these things in order to sound convincing, and also for her to continue to look after my washing.

Solange dried her tears, held me tightly against her large bosom, and told me I was an adorable little girl, that my father did not know how lucky he was, and that truly I deserved my Sunday treats.

Solange, please forgive me.

I have always lived with a father AND a mother. They have jobs, enough money, friends, holidays, plans. They both speak French, have a state-of-the-art washing machine, and even have a woman who comes and does cleaning and ironing. We go away for a month in the summer and a week in the winter. On 31st December, mama raises her glass to the thirteenth and fourteenth months each year for which she is paid but which do not actually exist, and toasts the twelve months that have been and gone without, however, causing too much damage. Papa then gives her a handbag or some perfume. They like anniversaries and they like going abroad.

They are happy to have a child, because that way there will remain some trace of their passage on this earth, like a small piece of eternity.

So there. I have found something nice to say about them.

I am sorry, Solange.

Would you like to adopt me?

Another thing I ought to say about my parents: they have never beaten me. I know that there are children who are beaten, battered, tortured. But for me, the worst I ever received was a slap across the face.

This year, as it happens, my parents had some problems, some 'complications', with their holiday plans. They found themselves running around in circles at the last minute looking for a holiday let.

In the end, they secured a tiny studio apartment on the Mediterranean, in a new 'mushroom' town along the coast. One room, twelve square metres, and as for the sea view it would have to wait till next year. Even so, they only managed to get this accommodation because, as mama complained, 'someone has backed out at the last moment . . . So it's bound to be hideous!'

Papa consoled her:

'What does it matter? You'll be on the beach all day long!'

'And the evenings?'

'The evenings we'll go out.'

'And the little one?' asked Mama.

I quickly guessed that the 'extra convenience bed' proposed as a solution in the letting agreement only half-suited them.

They were at the end of their tether, worn out by the year they were having. And in case I did not fully grasp this, it was made clear to me every day. They needed 'to rediscover themselves', 'relearn how to love', and a lot of other obscure things, to which I paid less and less attention, as it became clearer and clearer that my presence was going to be a nuisance.

The reproaches accumulated. I walked around on tiptoe.

Then one evening I had an idea.

I had not spoken for two days. We were now in July. I stayed at home most of the day or went for long walks. I bought food for the evenings, and read, and wrote to Sophie and to Jean. I was becoming 'a well-behaved young lady', with, as papa pronounced, 'the prospect of entering third year well ahead'. Each morning, Mama left me plenty of money to buy books and sweets, and pay the swimming pool admission.

So one evening I said:

'What about the summer camp?'

My parents looked at each other. It was now 22nd July.

The next day, mama came home from the office with an air of defeat. 'Too late,' she announced to papa, who had got home early, and had run to open the door when he heard the lift. 'I made a hundred phone calls! Obtuse, all of these organisations. As if one child more would make any difference.'

'That's them all over,' said papa.

He had just been painting a golden picture for me of the summer camp where I would have a marvellous time, a fabulous August. 'With no parents! Loads of friends! Fun camp counsellors!' My ears were positively ringing with it all.

Now he added: 'And look at how much we were willing to pay them!'

'No cancellations expected,' muttered mama.

'But of course. Even a sick child, the parents are all too happy to rid themselves . . .'

He glanced at me furtively, and changed colour. 'What I mean is . . . They are happy to give their child the benefit of fresh air, and the opportunity to experience life in a group . . .'

I said nothing. Sophie had known since March that she was going to summer camp this summer.

I was given to understand that I should have thought of this a lot sooner, that it was the first time I'd ever expressed a desire to go off on holiday without them . . .

'Express a desire' – one of mama's favourite expressions.

Solange,

everything is fine here, thanks to you. But Sundays are dreadful, even worse than at home. Anyway, there is probably only one Sunday left to go, and it's not for another five days.

Next Sunday, we'll see what happens.

I will be sitting in my corner, with the dog, and won't move. The dog won't ask questions, and I'll make sure he stays with me.

When he came back from running around the fields, that first Sunday, I think he felt a bit guilty about leaving me alone for the whole afternoon. He rested a timid paw on me. I put my arms around him and cried myself to sleep. We spent another night outside, which I prefer. That night in particular, I really didn't want to go back inside, where I'd been pestered by people – as if they knew somehow that Solange was not there to watch over me, even from a distance.

Inside it smells bad, of old plastic, bleach and sun-cream. Outside smells of petrol, exhaust fumes, and chips decomposing in corners.

The smells are always the same. And so strong that even the watered grass no longer smells of anything, other than the litres of dog pee which there has been no rain to wash away.

My apologies, dog.

Solange, I am here on summer camp. The post-card you gave me this morning, with a picture of the motorway services – I sent it to my parents at home. I wrote:

> A souvenir of the motorway, where I am having a wonderful holiday.
>
> Your darling Lily.

There's even a letter box, in this village suspended above the tarmac. And phone booths. We are not cut off from the world here, don't you believe it. We're slap bang in the middle of things.

Just now, the dog was lying on the grassy bank that runs down to the motorway. His ears were twitching despite himself, pricking up and then lying back and then pricking up again, in constant agitation.

Then he sat up and started to groan, bobbing from one front paw to the other, without moving his trembling hindquarters from the ground. Anyone watching would have said he was about to spring forwards and race flat out across eight lanes of motorway.

He didn't know that I was just behind him, that I was watching him.

Had he known, he would not have allowed himself to tremble like that, or prick up his soft ears and sit looking expectant. He would not have groaned as he sometimes does, at night, when (just for a few minutes) all noise ceases, for no apparent reason. No cars passing by, no people. Even in the filling station, not a single pump making its usual humming noise.

These silences always wake me up. They are the only moments of proper night — not night really, of course, since the huge orange lights are switched off only at dawn, and the white neon of the service station continues to throw its pallid blotch over the car park.

It is at these moments that the dog leaves me to go off and howl. Then I go off and find him.

He jumps up on me and licks me, and starts running so that I'll chase after him. We often run around like this, at night, through the car park, over the meagre grass plots, in and out of the sleeping lorries with their curtained cabins.

Never has a passer-by asked us what we are doing. Are we not travelling, just like him?

After this running about, the dog quietens down. He is happy to go back to sleep, and I nuzzle up to his warmth again, my head against his quivering flank.

So, to go back to where I was, this time I called out to him. I don't want him to feel bad, his brown eyes to go lifeless, or glitter as though he's been crying.

I shouted 'Dog!' three times before he paid attention. He ended by turning his head, but without moving. It was I who went and sat down beside him on the grassy slope.

'What day are we?' he asked.

'The 16th.'

I said nothing more, but after a while I couldn't help adding: 'In any case, it's far too early. This is only the middle of the month.'

I was annoyed at myself for being so blunt with him, and I rested my hand on his neck, which is rough and muscular, where the hair gets matted. I was ashamed of the questions I wanted to ask him. I rephrased them every which way in my head so that they would not wound him.

'Would you like to go back home with them?'

He made as if to shrug his doggy shoulders, and turned his nose to the wind. His black nostrils, cold and shiny, were quivering.

Then, as if he had not understood my question, he said, 'I'm a dog, after all.'

I did not argue with this. Does being a dog make any difference?

Because I did not want to cause him any pain, and because we had a long and irritating day in the burning sun to get through, I proposed that tomorrow we might go and see the other side of the motorway services, past the restaurant and the suspended boutiques.

The dog looked at me with his good dog eyes.

He likes plans, and being told what we are going to do in the afternoon, or the next day. It takes really very little to persuade him not to post himself sentry-like on the grass bank, trembling and cocking his ear to what lies beyond the sounds of the world.

It's early morning.

With the coins I've picked up off the ground since the beginning of the week, I was able to treat myself to some chocolate from the vending machine; and I even bought a croissant for the dog.

Everything was going very well.

Until I went to greet Solange when she arrived to lift her metal shutters.

Solange informed me coolly that there is not a single Serbo-Croat among the people working in the restaurant kitchens.

I could feel my face getting redder and redder, and I ran off.

It was a joke, Solange. I said 'Serbo-Croat' so that he would be a real mystery, a real foreigner from far away. Two Vietnamese and an Arab really work in the kitchens, but then you would never have believed me, would you?

I have not seen Solange since yesterday morning.

I have good reasons, since the dog and I were off on an expedition to the other side of the motorway.

The dog was deeply disappointed, of course.

Because the other side is exactly the same as this side. In fact, you need to pay a lot of attention not to get confused. North and South, Right and Left, everything is turned upside down. Only Above and Below seem to remain themselves. To find the side you have come from, you must first remember on which side the plate glass was when you arrived. Then you take the suspended corridor in the other direction. It's a complicated business.

No use relying on the trees planted on either side, or the petrol pumps, or the games: they are all identical. A mirror world.

Fortunately there are the faces of the people, to tell you which side you belong to. But there again, everything depends on the people. Besides, if Solange did not exist it wouldn't matter what side I was on. North carriageway, south carriageway – it would be all the same.

Fine. But Solange I'd recognise without difficulty, wherever I was. The girl in the tobacconist, on the other hand, has a blonde beehive hairdo exactly like the girl in the tobacconist on the other side. And exactly like the girl with the vapid smile on the cover of all the TV magazines this week. The TV girl is motionless and made of glossy paper, that's how you can tell her apart from the other two.

The smells are also the same on both sides. Except I couldn't help noticing that the cleaning is less well done on their side. There are cigarette ends and litter under the sticky plastic seats and on the shelves in the phone booths. On our side, never for more than an hour.

Mrs Simão on our side always looks as if she was born to hunt down rubbish, day and night. She never says a word, and watches me with a suspicious but not unkind expression. I have no fear that she might mistake me one day for a piece of rubbish.

When we pass her, me and the dog, she keeps her eyes fixed on the dog's paws to see if they are leaving any tracks. At which the dog's ears go back, he curves his spine and starts walking on tiptoe like a circus horse. He takes rapid dainty steps, as if hoping that any water or trace of mud brought in from outside will not have time to settle on the floor. He is in luck, since there has not been a drop of rain for the past ten days.

In any case, the tiled floor always gets so dirty that as soon she finishes a section, Mrs Simão has to go back over it again a quarter of an hour later. I have a feeling that Mrs Simão will never have the time to go to Venice.

Today, the dog tried to get me to go over to the other side again. I said no. I think he'd like to move over there. Now every day he asks me what is today's date; soon he'll be asking the hour. I don't have a watch. He only has to look up at the clock. He got on my nerves so much this morning that I lost my temper.

'Why do you want to go to the other side?' He looked down his nose at me, as if I had just asked the world's stupidest question.

'Because I am smart.' He waited for a moment; no doubt hoping I was going to ask him what he meant. 'Because I am intelligent', he repeated. 'They will think I've been waiting for them, but they will be convinced I've been waiting for them in the exact spot where they left me.'

I continued to say nothing. I was burning to tell him that his vile owners with their ball-ball no longer even give him a thought, that he ceased to exist for them the moment their car doors slammed shut against him.

'They won't be expecting me to find them on the other side, where they'll be stopping on their way home. No way.'

As I continued to say nothing, he spelt it out for me: 'I have the brains of a dog.'

Poor dog, his doggedness made me feel unhappy and upset.

'In any case,' I said, 'it's now only the 18th.'

'But they weren't planning to go away for the whole month.'

When he started going off, a few days ago, I hoped he was waiting for his owners – in order to eat them. All three of them. Plus their callousness, and their idiocy: which makes five. And their new seat-covers, which makes six.

But I know he lacks the stomach for that. Has anyone ever seen a dog avenge himself on those who abandoned him?

Someone told me a story about a dog whose

master rowed him to the middle of a lake in order to drown him. The master pushed the dog overboard, and in his enthusiasm also managed to topple into the water himself. He couldn't swim. But he found himself being supported in the water and being guided back to the boat. So the dog saved his life. And humans weep to see a dog offering them a simple lesson in humanity.

What I want to know is this: did the man then try to drown the dog again?

In the end, the dog looked at me with curiosity, and said, 'What about you? Aren't you going to be waiting on the other side too?'

Nothing to report. I think I'm going to finish my notebook today. So that I won't be disturbed, I have made myself comfortable behind the service station. It smells of petrol, but I'm better off here than anywhere else. Nobody will come looking for me.

Except for the dog, maybe. He has gone over to the other side. I don't think he'll be coming back. He does not want to miss his owners on their way back. I'm afraid we had a falling-out about that.

Falling out was hard for both of us. He only has me in the world, I only have him. That's how it is.

With Solange it's different. Though I fell out with her too. So here I am, crying like a baby. Idiotic.

Never mind. Let the dog be a dog and Solange be a Solange. They are exhausting. The dog waits for owners. Solange gets angry with me. She thinks I lied to her for the fun of it. The dog remains a dog because he thinks he is intelligent.

74

Solange is Solange because she thinks I'm naughty and that she has been taken in by me. This must be what people mean by self-esteem.

If this were summer camp, I would write immediately to my parents to come and fetch me. I would have no self-esteem. Today, I have no esteem at all. Not for anybody. There's not much point in esteeming those who aren't here. As for those who are here, they're to be found suspended above a motorway trying to decide which side they should be on so that their lives might mean something.

As if their sense of direction depended on the direction of the carriageway.

The dog hasn't an ounce of brains. I would tell it to him straight if he were here to be told. He has only the cunning of a slave who wants to get back into the good graces of his master.

As for me, I have no esteem for anyone or anything.

I don't think I love my parents. I stayed with them because I was small and they were convenient. Because I couldn't manage without them. They have shown me that now I'm big enough to be alone. Convenient. That is what they were.

When you are small, you have to find a reason which explains why you do not resemble your parents. So, of course, you decide on adoption. It is somehow reassuring.

Later on, you must have the courage not to find a reason. Or to tell yourself that it's because parents resemble no one. Or that they resemble the rest of the world.

This world they always seemed to want me to swallow whole, to the point of indigestion.

Parents resemble the world. Not all parents, of course. I'm aware of that. But mine do. Sophie's parents or Jean's parents resemble themselves. Gentle, encouraging, funny, clever (in ways unlike the dog). Maybe I should ask them to adopt me.

To start with, however, I ought to go to the police and notify them that I've lost my parents.

I arrived here three weeks ago.

The car went into a pond and disappeared. I told nobody. I was traumatised. Solange can bear witness: so traumatised that I made up outlandish stories to convince myself – if no one else – that my parents were next door all the time, in the restaurant, working in the kitchen.

A search party will be organised.

Naturally I have forgotten the location of the muddy pond. And even were I to recognise the place, it will be so deep and so pitch-black that they'll be quite unable to erect a winch or send down frogmen.

How did it happen?

Well, I got out of the car to have a pee. The car had stopped beside the pond. Suddenly it started sliding, and I watched as it slid slowly down into the slime.

Solange will be ashamed of herself for not guessing the tragedy I have been part of – unable to save my cherished parents.

She will take me home to her house and I'll sleep in a proper bed. I'd like a proper bed.

She will clutch me to her large bosom and sob loudly, thinking of all those Sundays and those evenings when she was not at the motorway services to watch over me.

No. Better still, they've been murdered.

Occupied as I was in embellishing this account of my vanished parents, I found that Sunday passed more quickly than usual. Even given the absence of the dog.

They were murdered.

The murderer had a hood and a chainsaw, but when he saw that he could not plug in the chainsaw (we were in the middle of a forest and the electricity was too far away), he took out a big knife, and a pistol and an axe.

He chopped my parents to pieces before they had time to say Help! I myself saw nothing, because I was perched in a tree and had closed my eyes. Like when something bad is happening on television, and mama and papa say in chorus: 'Close your eyes, Lily.'

Except that when I close my eyes I can still hear the sounds, and I can hear all those noises that tell me I'd be far better off keeping my eyes open.

I closed my eyes, Lily.

When there was no more noise at all, I climbed down from the tree and walked and walked, until I came to the motorway. I followed the cars, until I came to the services, which is where I've remained ever since.

'Traumatised, clearly,' the police officer will say. 'But where is this wood?'

'Traumatised,' the psychologist will say. 'You can see for yourself that she's in no condition to find the wood again!'

They will conclude that the murderer made off in the car.

The only problem, unfortunately, is the car.

Even I am aware that when the police look for a car with a registration plate, they always end up finding it. Result: they also find my parents inside it, or in close proximity. Alive and very well.

Perhaps I could send them another postcard:

Change your registration plate
immediately.
The police are looking for you
for murdering me . . .

Fond memories.
Your Lily who wishes you well.

But the fools will take it into their heads to go to

the nearest police station and say they've not murdered me, and 'What else have you been making up, Lily?'

The psychologist will conclude that the child is in any event irredeemably depraved.

I was once told as much, or at least papa and mama were told as much in front of me. Because they dragged me to see loads of doctors in loads of hospitals, to find out why I was vomiting so often. And after the results of endless tests and examinations, all of which said I was as right as rain, mama took me to a child psychologist.

It wasn't that mama thought I was crazy, she was just afraid that I was in a bad way, that we were all in a bad way on account of having to live together, them and me.

The psychologist advised a course of psychotherapy, since he found me disturbed, anxious, and delicate. I was in luck: he was too booked up to see me, so he sent me to one of his colleagues. She gave me back my freedom after three sessions because she found me well balanced, intelligent, and very mature. She suggested a course of psychotherapy for my parents. They replied that if I was well there was no earthly need.

So, no postcard, and no declaration to the police about lost parents.

This is all far too complicated.

The dog resurfaced yesterday evening. I caught sight of him at the end of the corridor. He was wearing his hangdog look. I don't like it when he puts on this expression, when he seems to be carrying the burden of the world on his back, the whole world breaking his back. He had even forgotten to walk on tiptoe to show Mrs Simão that he was not going to add to the dirt on her tiles.

He came up to me, slowly, his ears pinned back.

'Did you get bored, then, dog?'

I think he mostly had difficulty getting enough to eat. They are not so keen on dogs, on the other side.

I said nothing. I know that with me he can always eat as much as he wants, and even get by without the odd kick in the ribs.

I lied. The dog doesn't talk. The dog has never spoken a word.

He has never spoken, but he does speak with his eyes. His nice big deep watery dog's eyes, colour brown.

Dear parents, it is hard not loving you any longer.

Perhaps tomorrow I'll start to love them again. The month is nearly finished. My notebook too.

How difficult remorse is! They have come back, two days earlier than expected.

Their car is in the car park, on the other side. I've not spotted them, as yet. They will wander this way and that, looking for me, crossing from one side to the other, like people who cannot remember where their luggage locker is at the railway station.

Beyond the metal crash barriers which line the motorway, huge fields stretch to the horizon. I had not noticed them until today; I had stayed in the enclosure, the luggage locker in which they had deposited me. I was in a state of waiting.

Yes, I was waiting for you, because I thought I was too small to have no one in my life, no one responsible for me. Now I am responsible for me.

The world will be as in my dreams, without dogs like the dog, without people like you.

Huge fields stretch to the horizon. Very far off I

can see a steeple, the roofs of a village, which has the look of a real village, papa.

That is the direction I'll set off in. Perhaps I'll run into the dog out there, wandering up and down. Perhaps he will have thought things over.

No goodbyes, please. Since he came back to our side, he bays at the moon, which is full, but the moon does not respond.

His ears are still trying to catch the sounds beyond this world. His sides are hollow. He cannot sleep without whimpering, without wrestling with his demons. I watch him as he lets himself be eaten away by sorrow, as if by vermin.

In the middle of the fields, suddenly I will hear a racing sound, a sound of panting. I will turn around and see his big black fleecy body, bounding along through the corn, his big frame alive and stronger than the wind when it bends the swollen ears of corn this way and that, as it pleases.

The Beach

'Lily! Yoo-hoo, Lily!'

After she'd heard her name called four or five times, Lily raised her head, and her dark eyes seemed to return from far away before they focused on the shore – or rather, on what took the place of the shore on an August afternoon: an uninterrupted ribbon of near-naked bodies stirring constantly this way and that, along the fringe of waves and wet sand.

The bodies had reddened, then browned, over three weeks or more. Hardly elegant as yet, and slightly awkward still, like creatures that have yet to reach adulthood.

Among all the waving arms, the faces pleated by the sun, the multitude of yelling mouths, Lily was reluctant to seek out those who were seeking her out.

She put the cap back on her pen, however, and carefully stowed the large notebook in the canvas bag, which had left a white mark on her knees.

Once the notebook was tucked away in its canvas shelter, Lily let the world come roaring back and invade her with its noises and smells, its sand warm to the touch, its taste of hot sun.

The world washed back in shrill complainings from the beach, in the remains of marshmallow coated with sand, in the litter of empty tin cans.

Someone lay down quickly on the beaded matting to one side of Lily. Another body followed suit on her other side.

'Is everything OK, darling?'

A female hand stroked her light-brown hair.

'Yes,' said Lily.

'You're not going for a swim?'

'No, don't feel like it.'

'Really!' interrupted the voice of her father, from the other side. 'To spend an entire month by the sea and not get into the water once! Staying in that cramped room, or confining yourself to two square metres of sand when you have the whole beach! If you aren't going to swim or amuse yourself, I don't know why we brought you here!'

'Let her be,' said the mother softly, in a concil-iatory voice.

There was a silence between the three of them, a lingering silence, of an unusual kind, in which the conversation of the people around them could be heard. A silence nevertheless.

'Let it be!' cried someone else's mother, a few feet away, slapping the hand of her baby who had picked up something dirty in the sand.

'Let me be . . .' grumbled a man, exhausted by his wife rubbing him with sun-cream for the fiftieth time.

'Leeeash!' screeched an adolescent, whose dog had just taken off at full pelt into the distance.

Lily turned her head towards her mother, who was stretched out on her stomach, her eyelids half-closed.

The maternal voice resumed, just as caressing, just as understanding:

'Our Lily has been very busy this month. Isn't that so, Lily?'

She did not wait for the murmur of assent, which took its time coming.

'Lily has been writing. Isn't that right, Lily? And writing is a very absorbing activity . . .'

More silence.

'Are you writing up your journal, darling?'

Lily barely had time to be startled by this.

'But what's the point in keeping a journal if you aren't doing anything!' exclaimed the father. 'In a journal, you describe what you've done, not what you've not done!'

'You are so stupid, sometimes,' replied the mother. 'You also describe what you feel, what you think . . . Isn't that so, Lily?'

'_____'

'Or perhaps you have been writing a tale for us?' suggested the mother again.

'A fairy tale?' added the father, rather pleased with himself.

'A tale of a thousand and one nights?' added the mother, raising the stakes.

'An itemised account?'

By now they were both laughing.

'Or a settling of accounts, perhaps?' ventured the mother slowly, in a sleepy voice.

Still she had not opened her eyes.

Lily continued looking at her, in a sort of stupor, her heart beating very fast.

And the beach continued to make its overcrowded rustling murmur.

And the sea kept rolling its tarnished waves onto the beach.

Coming Back

The family packed and left the seaside next morning.

'We're leaving on Saturday morning, 6 a.m. on the dot, while it's cool!' the father had announced a few days earlier.

But when they began moving around at 4 a.m., in their miniscule apartment, the building was already reverberating with the noises of early risers. Quite a number of holidaymakers were taking the road home that day. In the cool.

The first thing Lily did on waking was to slide her hand under the pillow. Her warm fingers, a little swollen from sleep, encountered the cloth of the spine and then the soft laminated cover of the notebook. Safely in its place.

The shower was running in the bathroom. The sound of cups, the smell of coffee coming from the kitchen.

Her parents' sofa bed was already folded back into place, so that they could move around and pack the suitcases. At night, between the sofa transformed into a bed and the extra mattress laid out on the tiled floor, you could not take a single step in the room. The dining table and chairs were now folded and put away in the corners.

It was still dark.

No light was switched on in the bedroom-sitting-dining room, but the glow from other sources – the pallid kitchen light, the yellowish bathroom light through the half-open door – blended to reveal the outlines of furniture, and a disorder of clothes and other effects beside the three empty suitcases open on the sofa.

Reassured by the familiar sounds, and by the still-empty suitcases, Lily stretched out and remained lying on her back, her eyes on the ceiling.

The question that briefly prevented her from falling asleep the night before was tormenting her still, and demanding an answer: namely, would she or would she not write the word END at the foot of the last page of the notebook which, in the space of three weeks, she had covered with her story – her true untrue story – in round handwriting?

She was quite pleased with her invention, thanks to which the family summer, the overcrowded summer, the sweltering summer – the summer, all in all – had passed by.

Was it time to write the word END?

Secretly, Lily wanted her story to end. Rereading certain passages made her feel sad. As if, sometimes, the words and sentences had run ahead of themselves and taken off, outrunning her thoughts, pounding along the pale mauve lines of her notebook on their spindly legs. Outrunning reality itself.

And the monstrous evidence was right here, under Lily's warm pillow . . . How was it possible that, between these straight lines, pale and mauve, these virgin pages, there could have gushed forth this story of *anxiety* and *lonely uncertainty*; and did those three words rhyme with each other (this now occurred to her) so as to bind her all the more resoundingly to her precious but painful secret made of ink and paper?

Pushing away the bed-sheets with her foot, Lily made up her mind.

She would write the word END. And the notebook would be put away, forgotten about. Thrown away, even.

End of a made-up summer holiday diary. Life would begin again on the other side of this curious and disturbing hiatus.

In the bathroom, the shower had stopped. The electric coffee-maker was broadcasting its final hiccups and splutterings. The familiar sounds. Reliable and reassuring.

And yet . . .

Lily suddenly sat up straight on her mattress.

Something was wrong. She was certain of it, even before she was able to identify the confused source.

Nobody was singing or muttering in the bathroom or kitchen. No blundering early-morning hand was clattering cups, or slamming the refrigerator door. It was as if a muffle had been placed over all ordinary everyday sounds. Only the bathwater and the coffee machine sounded like themselves. All other movements were happening in slow motion: sparing, subdued, measured out.

Too subdued for comfort.

By now seriously worried, Lily got dressed.

The suitcases were there, for sure, and the parents too, inevitably. But why this silence, this sudden parsimony of movement? Had there been a quarrel? A drama of some kind? An upset?

Someone has died, Lily said to herself. Or someone is about to die.

But she immediately remembered that there was no phone in their room, that the postman had not yet called. No, bad news could not have arrived in the night and burrowed its way into their cosy home. An argument, then, concluded Lily.

At any moment, perhaps, papa's voice would boom out from the bathroom 'Venice!' and her mother's face would appear smiling at the door of the kitchen, a smile to obliterate the reddened eyes, the drawn features, the ageing face beneath the exaggerated tan.

Lily waited.

Nothing.

She took a step in the direction of the kitchen, but changed her mind and, noiselessly in her turn, started to dismantle the bed and place the mattress upright against the wall.

Then she simply stood there, feeling a bit helpless.

No one came out of the bathroom or out of the kitchen, which she now preferred not to enter. The pressure of these unseen silent presences was beginning to unsettle her.

The floor tiles were cold under her naked feet. She looked around. Noticing her clothes in a heap at one end of the sofa, she began to pack them into the smallest of the three suitcases, carefully, together with her books, her pencil case. The only thing missing was her toothbrush. She would fasten the suitcase after she had taken her shower. She slipped the notebook into the precious canvas bag that she always kept with her.

She had left out a pair of bermudas, a shirt, panties, her sandals.

In the kitchen, water was being splashed

around the metal surface of the sink. A cup was being rinsed. Then, in a silence barely disturbed by the rubbing of a dishcloth, Lily supposed her mother was drying the cup. The cupboard door opened, the cup knocked against a saucer, the door banged shut.

Her ears straining towards these sounds, trying to decipher the strangeness behind this facade of normality, Lily mustered her courage and stepped into the kitchen.

Her mother's back was turned; she was already dressed, her hair arranged, ready to leave. No doubt she was aware that she was no longer alone.

She turned round very quickly.

Never had Lily seen this face, defeated, worn out, pale despite the suntan, to which the intense lustre of the pupils and the bitter fold of the mouth seemed to give disturbing life.

Lily was as if paralysed. 'Hello . . . good morning, mama', she stammered.

The ensuing silence seemed to stiffen further the hostile mask of her mother.

'Are you not . . . is there any milk left?' asked Lily.

Unlike on other mornings, she could not see the bowl of milk steaming on the table, the two slices of buttered baguette on either side.

The reply, when it came, was brutally abrupt:

'Since you are so big, since you no longer need us, you can make your own breakfast.'

After which her mother left the kitchen, without glancing at Lily, without saying another word.

Lily at once understood everything.

She had betrayed herself. She had been betrayed. She had been a traitor.

She heated the milk, even though she no longer wanted it, just to be able to stay in the kitchen, to hold onto some vestige of normal life, for a few more moments, some remnants of life as it was before.

Before the notebook.

She gave a start when her father came into the kitchen, freshly shaven, scented, his hair washed and combed.

'So, our little budding writer, we take up our pen to invent monstrosities, do we?'

His eyes scanned Lily as if he did not see her, although he was addressing her — as if she were not there. He proceeded to pour himself a large bowl of coffee.

'I won't even mention the dishonesty, the lies. Where did you learn to write these disgusting things? These defama . . . these diffam . . . these deform . . . these slanders?'

'You read my notebook!' gasped Lily.

This time her mother replied, from the bedroom-sitting-dining-room.

'And it's fortunate that we did! I prefer at least to know that I have a shrew, a small nasty bug in my house!'

She came back into the kitchen, to bestow on her daughter not just the look of cool indifference one reserves for utter strangers, but also the look of hot accusation reserved for traitors.

The mother scrutinised this serpent she had brought forth and nursed at her breast, who now judged her so mercilessly, at the end of the long subterranean secret path along which love is mysteriously lost.

The Trial of Lily unfolded over the course of eight hundred kilometres and ten hours. Because quite a few holidaymakers had opted to set out 'in the cool of the morning', and because the Fourvière Tunnel experienced, as it always does, severe difficulty in digesting their numbers.

Lily did not say a word.

Her parents, by turns prosecutors, lawyers, judge, jury, victims, and witnesses, did it for her.

So she remained completely silent.

While in the front of the car there were tears and protestations, followed by lengthy monologues on the themes of ingratitude, cowardice, hypocrisy.

Lily remained completely silent.

She had played with the idea of a collapsed world, as an invention, as in a game, and here was her world collapsing.

She remained completely silent.

Because she was twelve years old, and it is a terrible thing to cause so much pain and wreak such havoc when you are twelve years old.

Lily remained silent because she had nothing more to say, as if her notebook, into which she had plunged each day, had in turn abducted her from all that is reassuring, all that is comforting, and forced her to grow up so quickly — too quickly? — at whatever cost.

Lily turned these things over and over in her mind, while the trial in the front seat followed its course. She ended by telling herself that twelve years was a good age to grow up, and to grow up in one big leap.

'Let's start again from the beginning,' suggested Sergeant Boudu.

He put his hand on his head and hesitated, as if still surprised not to find the silken tangle of hair that had deserted his bald crown these twenty years or more.

Boudu lowered his clear, curiously mild eyes, to steal a glance at the jotter on which he had made some notes.

The story so far was a trifle confused.

'So, you arrived at the motorway services on Saturday, 25th August – in other words the day before yesterday – at approximately 4 p.m.'

Opposite him, two tearful visages nodded in simultaneous agreement.

'You were coming from the seaside and were returning to the Paris region.'

Renewed nodding from the two haggard faces. The woman added a sniffle and held a handkerchief to her reddened nose.

'You arrived, you parked the car in the car park, not far from where the video games are situated, as you have said, and all three occupants got out of the car . . . I'll skip the minutiae – seeing to nature's needs, cafeteria break, driver purchases newspaper, and so forth.'

'A weekly paper,' added the driver, helpfully.

Sergeant Boudu looked at him wearily. 'Whatever you say,' he muttered.

He remained still for a moment in contemplation of his notepad, as if waiting for a ray of inspiration to burst forth from it; some dazzling light that would spirit him away from this tedious report.

Either he had sauce for brains or this couple were not telling the whole truth. He pressed on. 'And it was at this point, you say, that you became aware of the disappearance of your daughter.'

The woman hesitated for a second before nodding in agreement.

'Absolutely!' exclaimed the husband, a little over-zealously.

'So, you searched for her . . .'

'Yes! For an hour!' interjected the man.

'For two hours and ten minutes!' contradicted the woman. 'It was nearly six o'clock when we left.'

'Quite so,' retorted Boudu. 'That is what bothers me. Why did you leave?'

'To look for her!' they exclaimed in unison.

'To look for her? To look for her?' repeated the sergeant. 'But the motorway services were the place to look for her, since it was at the services that she disappeared.'

The parents looked at the ground sheepishly.

'Yes, but . . .' the woman stammered. 'We thought that . . . we thought we might find her in one of the neighbouring villages . . .'

'A peculiar notion,' said Boudu pointedly. 'Given that it's a fair distance to the nearest village, even cutting across the fields . . .'

'Unless she set off straight after we arrived,' suggested the father. 'Since we spent two hours looking for her, she would have had plenty of time to reach the village . . .'

'Hold it right there.' The sergeant stopped him. 'If I follow you correctly, you are not thinking of a straightforward disappearance, but a sort of . . . voluntary disappearance. That she ran away, to put it bluntly?'

The mother gave a start, and reddened. Boudu looked at her.

'Something makes you think she could have run away?' he enquired softly.

Silence.

'You say that she is only twelve years old, yes?'

The father nodded.

'It could be a case of abduction, of course,' suggested Boudu, slowly.

The mother began sobbing. The husband placed a hand on her shoulder. Boudu sighed loudly.

'Let us get to the point . . .'

He paused for a moment, letting his pale gaze wander around the antiquated interview room. Soon he would put in for a transfer, before retirement. He had no desire to end his days on a beat consisting of a motorway service station: a makeshift population that permitted itself every sort of excess.

The previous month, he and his men had had to go and fetch a little old lady whose family had abandoned her while she went to the washrooms. Impossible in such cases to track down the owners. The family rather.

More or less senile, the old woman was unable to give the address of her children. She repeated endlessly a first name, that of her son – when she wasn't conversing with her dead husband.

She was convinced, moreover, that she'd been brought to a Club Méditerranée, and probably took the policemen to be some of those nice young activity leaders in disguise.

Since no one knew what to do with her, she was deposited in a hospital in Dijon, and in spite of the appeals put out locally and nationwide, on television, nobody had come to claim her. Naturally she carried no papers – not even a collar such as dogs have. Sometimes.

And now this kid.

Sergeant Boudu sighed once again.

'You waited almost forty-eight hours before reporting the disappearance of your little girl. Why?'

Both parents felt transfixed by his mild inquisitorial gaze.

'But . . . it's like we said. We were looking for her!'

'Come, come! This is frankly ridiculous!' Boudu exploded. 'You do not head off on your own in search of a stray daughter for forty-eight hours. Have you given any thought to what might have happened to her during that time?'

The mother started sobbing with renewed vigour. 'Please find her, I beg you! Bring our Lily back to us!'

As for the outburst of maternal distress, Sergeant Boudu preferred to reserve judgement.

There was something very odd about these two.

'Let's go back over the hypothesis that she ran off . . .'

The subsequent police investigation cast immediate doubt upon the claims of the parents: according to enquiries made in the surrounding villages, it seemed that the couple had not shown their faces thereabouts (and villages have a way of knowing everything, more or less); that consequently the man and woman could not have questioned anyone to discover if a little girl had been seen passing through. Which naturally invalidated the forty-eight hours of alleged searching.

On the other hand – and this was by no means a negligible detail – the grocer's wife in the village nearest to the motorway services stated that she had noticed a small girl crossing the main street early on Saturday evening.

She remembered quite clearly that it was 7 p.m. and she asked herself where this solitary child might be heading. The little girl was wearing red bermudas and a dark green short-sleeved blouse, with a canvas bag across her shoulder, and she was walking along without apparent exhaustion, her eyes fixed straight ahead, as if she knew exactly where she was going.

'As if she knew exactly where she was going!' repeated the witness several times. It is not every day that a sleepy village sees a small traveller passing through with a firm step, asking nothing of anybody.

Another detail struck the grocer's wife: when the little girl stepped onto the pavement, a dog had barked – no doubt the dog from the Trochu farm, who never sits still for five minutes. The child had swung around sharply and called out: 'The dog!' Her eyes remained fixed for a moment on the far end of the street. Then she shrugged her shoulders and kept on walking.

The second hitch was that the three policeman who had gone off to investigate matters at the motorway services returned with some astounding information. During the entire course of Saturday afternoon, nobody had reported the suspected disappearance of a little girl.

'As you can imagine, we're used to lost children here,' the tobacconist had said, 'and the news would have done the rounds of all the shops pretty quickly! It often happens that a kid wanders off, just like in department stores, but they're always found again in five minutes. Mostly it's because they've got the two sides of the carriageway confused!

At which point, noted the policeman in his report – for he was a conscientious policeman, and neglected no detail – the tobacconist had fallen silent, looked to the left and right, scanned with her impassive painted eyes the long corridor spanning eight lanes of asphalt, and then scrutinised the entrances of the two cafeterias on either side of the sort-of bridge.

'It's true – they *are* identical,' she murmured. Astonishment muffled her voice, in which there stirred a note of anxiety. 'How are you meant to tell one side from the other . . . unless you're from here all along?'

She came out of her reverie, and seemed suddenly to remember the existence of the policeman who was questioning her.

'Of course, no one is really from here. I have simply got used to the place. I only need to remember that I turn right after lowering the shutters.'

The policeman went off, making for the wrong side as he did so. He was recalled by the voice of a colleague: 'Hey! Come and take a look at this!'

He turned his head and then turned on his heels. The colleague was crouching eye-to-eye with the tubs of artificial flowers flanking the entrance to the restaurant.

He had already deposited at his feet the fruits of his expedition into the maze of plastic undergrowth: cigarette ends, chewing gum, a whole heap of unidentifiable trifling rubbish.

This plunder was not what interested him. His groping fingers had just fastened onto an object, flat, smooth, quite large. He pulled it towards him.

It was a notebook, fairly thick, with a purple cloth spine and laminated covers. A notebook whose pages were covered in a round childish hand.

The first page was blank on both sides, after the fashion of meticulous schoolchildren.

At the top of the third page a date was inscribed, and neatly underlined, though you could tell from one or two minor wobbles that it had not been traced with a ruler:

Tuesday, 31st July

Yesterday, as soon as we got here, they started to behave weirdly . . .

The police station was no longer submerged in its usual sleepy routine. There was an atmosphere of crisis, drama, upheaval.

On one side of the table sat Sergeant Boudu, his elbows resting on his blotter, his hands joined. On the other side, the parents of little Lily.

Between them, in the centre of the table, lay the notebook with the purple cloth spine. Boudu had spent half the night reading it and rereading it, to make sure he understood everything. Late in the morning, he had summoned the parents to come down from the village inn.

As soon as she entered the interview room, and saw the purple notebook, the mother had a fit of hysterics. The father turned very pale.

The sergeant requested a glass of water for the woman, and then ordered the door of the office to be shut, so as to be alone with the couple.

For Boudu, it was the last time that this door would be closed on his orders. Tomorrow, he had decided, he would resign. He would make do with a meagre pension, cultivate his garden, distil brandy from his own plum trees, and above all – above all – try his hand at photography, which he had always longed to do. Wedding photos, taken when people are happy, or at least when they radiate the illusion of being happy. After more than thirty years of service, Sergeant Boudu had come to prefer faces on paper – matt or shiny, black and white or colour – to those he had watched file past him: haggard, fearful, defeated, faces endlessly distorting and recomposing. The whole human condition in the twisted fold of a mouth, in a fleeting glance.

From now on, he only wanted to see human faces on coated paper. While they were posing. The only time in their lives when they are presentable.

Such were his thoughts as he steered the interrogation briskly to its conclusion, with textbook severity.

'This diary . . . are we to believe, then, that you did in fact abandon your daughter at the motorway services on 30th July last?'

This provoked from across the table an outburst of cries, protestations, justifications, to which he lent only half an ear.

The father threw out his chest to show that he held firm in adversity, the mother poured forth her woes to the point of prostrating herself on the floor, which was white from having been bleached so frequently.

Bleach was what was needed, thought Boudu, to get rid of all the traces.

'You may well have murdered her into the bargain.' Thus Boudu.

'Are you insane?' the woman began shrieking.

'Stop now. Shush! Calm yourself!' shouted her husband.

Boudu waited while her cries died slowly down.

'You are lucky', he continued in a calm voice, 'that no one working at the motorway services is called Solange. On the other hand, the two tobacconists do have a blonde beehive hairdo, just like the blonde on the cover of the current TV magazines. But we'll let that pass . . .'

Confronted by the look of shattered dismay on the faces of the parents, he had to suppress a smile.

'Moreover, all the employees at the motorway services are in agreement that no little girl has been haunting the premises for the whole of August . . . even though the cleaning woman, who

– luckily for you once again, is not called Mrs Simão – confirms that someone did walk off with one of her large bin-bags . . .'

The father and mother had by now ceased exclaiming and protesting and changing colour, in order to listen with all ears to these assuaging words.

'The last troubling detail, but which neither incriminates you nor proves your innocence: the grocer's wife who saw your daughter walking through the village says that the child had an air of looking for a dog which had been following her.'

Boudu paused for a moment.

'Here I will leave off interpreting events,' he concluded. 'I can also reassure you: I telephoned the local police where you say you spent your holidays. My colleagues made enquiries. There were indeed three of you occupying the holiday let. A couple with a child matching the description you gave me of your daughter . . .'

These last words fell into a silence, in which the father's sighs of relief could be heard vying with the final spasms of the mother.

'It is established therefore that your daughter, for whatever reason, became separated from you on the afternoon of 25th August. Two hours later, she was seen passing through the village nearest to the motorway services. And now – and now you are both going to tell me the truth about what happened.'

' . . . So you can imagine our state of despair when we discovered this notebook!'

'This disgusting notebook!'

'This tissue of lies!'

'This inquisition!'

'Something you would not credit a child with the capacity to invent!'

Sergeant Boudu listened.

He listened for a long while, patiently.

'Let us get to the point,' he said at last. 'Very well, so your daughter . . . invented a story, about being abandoned for the month of August at a motorway services. She wrote a made-up journal recounting this month of August. You then read her notebook . . . behind her back?'

'But of course! You should have seen how she brooded over it.'

'She would not be parted from it for one moment.'

'In the end we began to ask ourselves what she could be hiding that made her so distrustful of us!'

'Of us, her parents!'

'The night before leaving, we removed it from under her pillow . . .'

'We were not being inquisitive!'

'We just wanted to know . . .'

'It was perfectly legitimate . . .'

Faced with this avalanche of justifications, Boudu averted his attention, and merely asked:

'And then?'

'We only wanted to teach her a small lesson – by driving off.'

'Only a very small lesson!'

'But when we came back, two hours later . . .'

'After all, we're not monsters.'

'A tiny lesson!'

'When we came back, she was nowhere to be found.'

'It's true that we did not make enquiries.'

'We did not dare to!'

So they went back to their home, in the Paris region.

'We told ourselves that perhaps she had already made her own way home.'

'That she was paying us back!'

Then, finding no one at home, they drove back to the motorway services, before making up their minds – 'The truth, at last!' sighed Sergeant Boudu – to alert the authorities.

Beyond the metal crash barriers which line the motorway, huge fields stretch to the horizon. I had not noticed them until today; I had stayed in the enclosure, the luggage locker in which they had deposited me. I was in a state of waiting.

Yes, I was waiting for you, because I thought I was too small to have no one in my life, no one responsible for me. Now I am responsible for me.

The world will be as in my dreams, without dogs like the dog, without people like you.

Huge fields stretch to the horizon. Very far off I can see a steeple, the roofs of a village, which has the look of a real village, papa.

That is the direction I'll set off in. Perhaps I'll run into the dog out there, wandering up and down. Perhaps he will have thought things over.

No goodbyes, please. Since he came back to our side, he bays at the moon, which is full, but the moon does not respond.

His ears are still trying to catch the sounds

119

beyond this world. His sides are hollow. He cannot sleep without whimpering, without wrestling with his demons. I watch him as he lets himself be eaten away by sorrow, as if by vermin.

In the middle of the fields, suddenly I will hear a racing sound, a sound of panting. I will turn around and see his big black fleecy body bounding along through the corn, his big frame alive and stronger than the wind when it bends the swollen ears of corn this way and that, as it pleases.

Lily

'Lily! Yoo-hoo, Lily!'

Lily gave a start and looked up. Her fingers sifted the sand, automatically, taking a handful and letting it run between them; then she plunged her hand in again, deeper, down to where the sand was slightly damper, denser, heavier. This sand did not slide between her fingers as in an hourglass; it broke off in small lumps, shapeless and irregular.

Lily flung some honey-coloured grains.

'Yoo-hoo! Lily!'

She wiped her hand on the towel before putting the cap back on her pen, and carefully stowed the large notebook away in the canvas bag, which had left a white mark on her knees.

Her name was called again.

At the edge of the water two grown-ups were waving at her vigorously.

She waved her arms back at them.

They were shouting for her to come into the

water.

'Coming!' she replied loudly, cupping her hands so they might hear.

Not far away on the beach, a large black dog with long hair was stretched out asleep.

He was lying on his stomach, his head resting on his paws, which were ranged neatly together. His nose glistened. His floppy ears, oblivious for a moment to the world and its noises, were touching the sand, some grains of which had stuck to their irregular tips, which were damp and shining from having an instant earlier been submerged in the water.

Each day Lily had watched this dog, playing or sleeping near its owners.

There was a movement in the warm air, next to Lily. She opened her eyes and saw her mother bend down, take a towel, and raise it to her dripping face.

Now her eyes were visible again, bright, smiling.

'Is everything OK, my darling?'

Lily nodded. Just now, she had a longing to dive into the water, to let the waves carry her, to taste the salt on her lips, and to feel on her skin the icy thrill of the sea after the heaviness of the sun.

In the evening the family went to a restaurant. They were due to leave next morning.

'At six o'clock,' said her father. 'On the dot!'

'In the cool of the morning!' said Lily, winking at him.

Her father seemed taken aback, for just a second, then he laughed and ruffled her hair.

'That's right, you minx!'

Now Lily laughed, and her mother too, but then Lily's eyes started to prick. With no warning, which was cowardly of them. And at the same time a lump rose in her throat, which stopped her from swallowing the last morsels of raspberry ice-cream.

It was fortunate they were on their dessert, thought Lily. Because at the rate this spider of sadness was weaving his obstruction at the back of her throat, she would soon start to choke.

Her father emptied the last of the champagne into their glasses. They had decided to celebrate a little this evening, their last evening.

'A little more, Lily?'

With a tense smile, Lily nodded. She had already been granted a chill mouthful of the pale golden bubbles a quarter of an hour ago. Mama had held out her glass to hear its fake crystal chime against Lily's glass. There followed a series of tiny tinklings, like the peal of distant bells.

For the sake of the occasion, rather than because she relished the taste, Lily accepted a further drop.

It was eleven o'clock when they left the restaurant.

Outside, the halyard ropes were knocking against the metal masts of the yachts dozing at anchor in the port.

'One day I would like to set off in a boat,' said her father, stopping in front of the slipway that shone in the black water.

Lily had a sudden impression that all the noises of the city had stopped – the passing cars, the hubbub on the café terraces, the laughter of people strolling in groups.

'Perhaps we shall,' said her mother, taking her husband's hand.

'Perhaps never,' he replied.

His voice was low, because voices always sound subdued when they are traversed by dreams. Not the ordinary desire for a boat trip, but the unquenchable longing to drift, far beyond land-fall, to the edge of things.

And then, suddenly, Lily understood that Venice or Bora-Bora were just reassuring words for grown-ups, letting them believe that their dream has a country, a homeland, complete with cities, beaches, lagoons, gondolas and palm trees. Since the spider at some point weaves his heavy ball at the back of all our throats.

No, one ought to dream more deeply, more boldly, differently, for everyday life to become liveable and full. Not dreams of escape . . . but dreams committed to paper, or realised in other ways, to be able to say to yourself that, yes, after-wards the world will have changed a little.

They took a few more steps.

Her mother was still holding her father's hand. She turned around, stopped, held out her other hand to Lily, who was trailing behind. Lily took the hand and their fingers interlocked.

The halyards were still snapping in the breeze.

They had almost arrived home when her mother exclaimed: 'Your bag, Lily!'

'Eh?'

'Your canvas bag, with your notebook!'

'Oh . . .'

Lily no longer had it with her. It was hanging from the back of the chair in the restaurant.

'I'll go and get it,' said her father.

He went off, taking long strides. Running almost.

Lily watched him disappear. Passing in front of the port, he would be thinking again of the boat that would not be taking him away.

'Shall we go up?' said her mother.

They took the lift to the fourth floor.

While her mother was unfolding the sofa bed, Lily got straight into bed, on the extra mattress.

'Are you going to sleep?'

'Mmmm . . .'

'Aren't you going to wait for him to get back, to make sure your notebook isn't lost?' said her mother in a surprised tone.

'Not lost . . .' murmured Lily.

She was asleep.

It was still dark when Lily opened her eyes.

The shower was running in the bathroom. The sound of cups, the smell of coffee coming from the kitchen.

Her parents' bed was folded up, the suitcases open on top of it, already packed.

The canvas bag was on the floor against the front door of the apartment, a bag of uncertain white, its shoulder straps slumped over in a lifeless arabesque.

The familiar reassuring noises continued.

Lily sat up in the bed. Yes, the sounds continued, as if they had no reason ever to fall silent, ever to come to an end.

Her father was whistling in the shower. Her mother was muttering because the milk had just boiled over.

Lily smiled and, once again, her eyes were pricking. She stepped lightly down onto the tiles, cold beneath her bare feet. She went quickly to the canvas bag, brought it to the bed, felt inside for the violet-backed notebook, began to open it, but then changed her mind.

She had planned to add one page after the scene with the police sergeant. The final page:

Saturday, 25 August
I lied.

But that wasn't quite the word for it. It was not a case of truth or lies. She had merely held a distorting lens over certain memories, certain inventions, and let her imagination play around with some obscure regions of sadness in her life. That was all.

The notebook went back into its canvas shelter.

Lily stood up again and pushed open the kitchen door. A large steaming white bowl was waiting for her on the table. Framed by two buttered lengths of baguette.

'Hello, mama,' Lily said.

Her mother turned around and kissed her forehead.

'Hurry up and eat. Your father is anxious to leave.' She continued cleaning the electric hob.

'Departure in two minutes!' said her father, as he shot out of the bathroom. 'Lily – into the shower!'

He was in the kitchen, swallowing a mouthful of warm coffee. 'I found your bag, did you see?'

Lily said, 'Yes, thank you,' before taking a sip of her milk.

Her heart was beating quickly.

She wanted to hide herself in her father's arms, in the arms of these people who were her parents, to ask their forgiveness for having written such things about them in a notebook. Awful things. Which were not true, or not exactly true – and what did it matter anyway?

In a flash, Lily understood that one day she would be their age, would lead their life perhaps, inherit the same world, more or less.

Having felt the shocks, having fingered the cracks in the porcelain, would Lily not make them her own, if only to go on living and get up each morning without too much pain? Then, in her turn, would she not put up with the accusations of her children, that they too, later on, may have a life woven out of renunciations, small mean-nesses, small triumphs, and shot through with flickering dreams that they try to commit to paper, so as not to lose sight of them for ever?

Having finished her milk, Lily stood under the shower. Five minutes later, she reappeared dressed. She grabbed her notebook, and went to the rubbish bin in the kitchen.

'What on earth are you doing?' asked her mother.

Lily had her hand on the cold handle of the bin, the notebook pressed to her chest.

She raised her eyes towards her mother's face, which looked tender at this moment, vaguely worried, a thousand things expressed in her brown eyes.

'I'm throwing it away.'

This was said in a distant, matter-of-fact voice, as if she were talking about some empty packaging.

'But why? You've spent a whole month writing in it, and now you want to get rid of it?'

'___'

'You'll regret it afterwards.'

'But it's no good! It's worth nothing!' exclaimed Lily, with a sudden flash of anger.

'That's what you think at this moment,' said her mother.

'You don't even know what's in it!' retorted Lily, as though issuing a challenge. And with an urge to clasp her arms tightly round her mother for not having pried into her secrets.

'But what does that matter?' said her mother. 'I don't know what it contains, but you do, and it's your notebook.'

The rubbish bin closed again with a rubbery muffled shutting noise, without swallowing the object.

'Into the car!' shouted her father, from the front door.

He had already loaded the suitcases.

In the kitchen, Lily was sobbing, her arms around her mother's waist.

'I don't want you to die,' she was saying.

'But I'm not going to die,' murmured her mother.

'Never!' cried Lily.

She had the feeling of being little again. Or on the contrary, of becoming very big. She was not bothered either way.

'Perhaps, one day . . .' said her mother. 'But we still have time.'

'Well then, we must stop dying a little every day,' pleaded Lily.

'Yes . . . yes . . .' stammered her mother.

'Even if it's only by writing in a notebook that it will not happen.'

'Yes, if you like, yes . . .'

'Into the car!' repeated her father.

It would never be his lot in this life to cry out: 'Get ready to cast off!' Was that his fault? A little. Not entirely. Not only.

'Into the car! We have to get to Lyon by eleven. Let's get moving!'